East of the Sun, West of the Moon

Retold by Susanna Davidson
Illustrated by Petra Brown

Reading consultant: Alison Kelly
Roehampton University

Contents

Chapter 1

The white bear

Far away to the north, where the land is covered in thick, dark forests and the wind blows bitterly cold, there lived a poor family.

Late one afternoon, they sat
huddled around the hearth.
The firelight flickered over the
children's faces.

The boys were handsome, the
girls pretty – but the youngest,
Asta, was the most beautiful of all.

As dusk began to close in around the cottage, there came a knock at the door. "Who's there?" called the father. But there was no answer.

So the father rose and opened the door, letting in a rush of icy air. Before him stood a towering white bear.

"I have watched your family all summer," said the bear, in a rumbling voice. "And I am ready to make you an offer."

"If you give me your youngest daughter," he went on, "I can make you as rich as you are now poor."

"I'll not give you my daughter," said the father, blocking the way, "however poor we may be."

But Asta looked into the sad, black eyes of the great white bear, and made up her mind.

"We barely have enough food to eat," she said. "And our clothes are turning to rags. How will we survive the winter? I will go with the bear."

So saying, she stood up, collected a small bundle of belongings and walked steadily to the door.

"Don't go!" cried her mother.

"The bear must be under a spell," she whispered in her daughter's ear.

"Don't worry, Mother," said Asta, "I am not afraid."

Asta climbed on
the bear's back.
"Keep a tight
hold of my fur,"
he told her.

Then, before anyone could
stop him, he bounded away
into the night.

10

Chapter 2

Inside the mountain

While the moon was still high in
the sky, Asta and the bear arrived
at a craggy black mountain.

11

The bear raised his huge paw
and knocked on the mountainside.
A door creaked open...

Inside, was a glittering castle,
carved from stone.

12

The white bear handed Asta a golden bell. "Ring this if you need anything," he said.

No sooner had Asta taken the bell, than she found herself alone in a grand bedroom. She lay down on the bed, but couldn't sleep.

Clouds passed over the moon,
sinking the castle into darkness.
Footsteps echoed down the corridor.
Asta peered out from her room,
and saw a man in the shadows.

He dragged behind him
a white bear skin, which
gleamed in the moonlight.

Each night after that, Asta
watched the man until he
disappeared into one of the rooms.
"Is that the bear, changed into a
man?" she wondered.
She longed to see his face.

The days rolled on. Asta had everything she could ask for. And, each evening, the bear would come and sit by her side. She would stroke his soft fur and sing to him.

The bear would rest his head on her lap, with a glimmer of hope in his dark eyes.

But Asta felt lonely in the castle, with the bear who rarely spoke. All day she would sit and wonder about the man who walked in the shadows.

The white bear watched the roses fade from her cheeks. "What is it?" he asked one day. "What do you want?"

"I want to go home," Asta
replied, "just for a day, to see my
family again."

"That can be arranged," said
the white bear. "If you will only
promise me not to talk to your
mother alone."

The next day, they set out on the long journey, with Asta astride the white bear's back.

At last they came to a large farmhouse. "This is where your family lives now," said the white bear.

"I will leave you for a night and a day. But don't forget what I said, or you will do much harm to us both."

Asta was filled with happiness to see her family again. But before she left, her mother managed to get her alone.

Asta soon told her about the man who paced the corridors at night – and how she'd never seen his face.

"You might be living with a troll!" her mother said. "You must take a candle. Hide it in your clothes and light it when he's asleep."

21

That night, Asta kindled her
light, then followed the man to his
room. She held it above his sleeping
form, and saw the handsomest
prince of her dreams.

Unable to resist, she bent down
and kissed his cheek. As she did
so, three hot drops of wax fell
upon his shirt.

The prince woke with a start. "What have you done?" he cried. "I've been bewitched by the troll queen, so I'm a bear by day and a man by night."

"I was to be set free if I could find a girl who would love me for a year... without seeing my human face."

"Now I must go to the
castle that lies east of the
sun and west of the moon.
And there I must marry
the troll queen."

"Can't I go with you?"
Asta begged.
"No," answered the prince.

24

"The troll queen has me under a powerful spell. I *must* go to her."

"Then I'll follow you there," vowed Asta.

"You can try," said the prince sadly, "but you'll never find me."

25

Chapter 3

Golden gifts

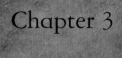

When Asta awoke the next
morning, both the prince and
the castle had gone.

She was lying in a forest clearing, with nothing but the clothes she came in. "I'll head north," Asta decided, "because that is where the trolls dwell."

Asta walked for many days and many nights, until her feet were sore and her legs were weary.

She thought of her last journey on the white bear's back – the feel of his thick, soft fur and the speed at which he bounded along.

"I'll never find him," she wept.

"You shouldn't give up so easily," croaked a voice. Asta looked up to see an old woman standing beside a horse.

"Can you help me?" Asta asked, eagerly. "I'm looking for my prince. He's in the castle that lies east of the sun and west of the moon."

"Aha!" said the old woman. "So you're the girl. I've heard tales of you and your search."

I will help you.

"I'll give you my horse and three golden gifts," she went on, handing Asta a comb, an apple and a pear.

"Where shall I go?" asked Asta. "To find the castle, ride until you meet the East Wind," the old woman said. "That is all I know."

Asta climbed on the horse's back
and the old woman whispered in its
ear. A moment later, they were off.

"Thank you!" called Asta, as
her voice was whipped away by
the wind.

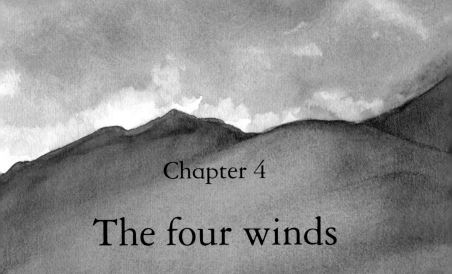

Chapter 4

The four winds

The horse's hooves pounded over the ground. Faster and faster he flew and Asta clung to his mane.

On a cliff top overlooking a rolling sea, the horse finally came to a stop. All around them, the East Wind blew in gentle gusts.

"Can you tell me the way to the castle that lies east of the sun and west of the moon?" Asta asked.

"I have never blown that far,"
the East Wind replied. "But I
will take you to my brother, the
West Wind. He may know
the way, for he is much
stronger than I."

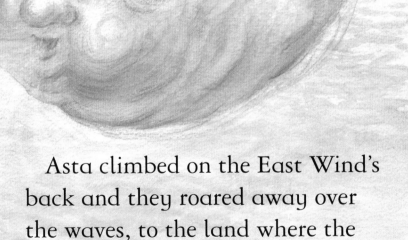

Asta climbed on the East Wind's
back and they roared away over
the waves, to the land where the
West Wind lived.

"Brother," called the East Wind, "do you know the way to the castle that lies east of the sun and west of the moon?"

"No," said the West Wind. "I have never blown that far. But I will take the girl to the South Wind, for he is much stronger than either of us and has roamed far and wide."

So they rode to the land where
the South Wind lived.

"Only the North Wind knows
the way to the castle," said the
South Wind, "for he is the oldest
and strongest of us all. I will carry
you there."

When they came near the North Wind, Asta felt his presence in the frantic, icy blasts of air.

"What do you want?" he roared.

"I carry the one who seeks the prince, in the castle east of the sun and west of the moon," the South Wind replied.

38

"I know it," said the North Wind. "I blew there once, but I was so tired that for many days after, I could not blow at all."

"If you are not afraid to go with me," the North Wind went on, "I will take you there."

Asta thought of her
prince with his sad,
black eyes. "I am not
afraid," she said.

Then the North Wind puffed
himself up, until he was so big and
strong he was frightful to see.

40

Asta climbed on his back and together they flew through the air, as if they would not stop until they reached the end of the world.

Below them, storms raged over the oceans and ships were tossed like toys on the roaring waves.

At last they had gone so far that
even the North Wind felt tired.
He sank lower and lower,
until the waves dashed
against Asta's feet.

"Nearly... there..." puffed the
North Wind, and with a final gust,
he blew her onto an icy shore.

42

Above her, east of the
sun and west of the
moon, rose the troll
queen's castle.

Exhausted, Asta crawled into a
cave beneath the crags, and slept.

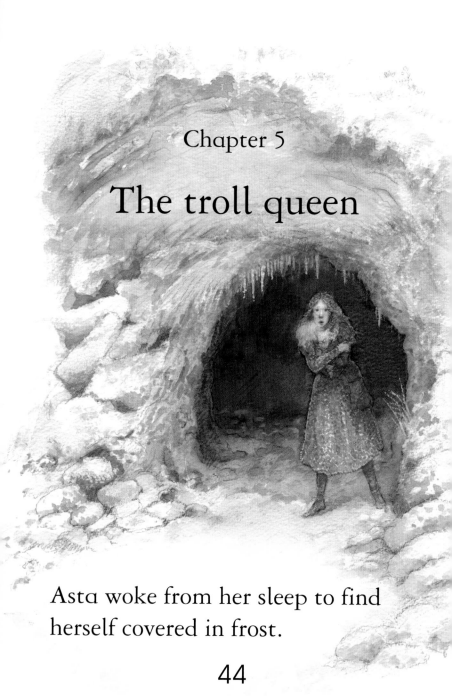

Chapter 5

The troll queen

Asta woke from her sleep to find
herself covered in frost.

With stiff limbs, she climbed
the crags to the castle door. From
behind a rock, she watched the
trolls lumbering in and out.

They carried buckets and mops,
rolls of red carpet and yards of
white silk.

"They're preparing for the wedding!" Asta gasped, and she slipped inside the castle to search for her prince.

The castle was filled with trolls... but her prince was nowhere to be seen.

46

Finally, she came to a grand room lit by candlelight. There, on a great stone throne, sat the troll queen herself.

She had string-like hair which she combed with long, yellow nails, and a nose that drooped down to her lap.

"What do you want?" she asked, in a voice like grinding stones. "I've come to see the prince," Asta replied.

The troll queen beckoned Asta closer. "First you must give me something in return," she said.

Asta looked down at her tattered clothes, then remembered the old woman's gifts. "I could give you this golden comb?" she said.

The troll queen grabbed it from her with a claw-like hand. "You may see the prince tonight," she snapped. "He's in the room at the top of the tallest tower."

That night, Asta rushed to the prince's room, and there she found him, fast asleep. She shook him and called to him but nothing would wake him.

In the morning, the troll queen returned. "Now get out of my castle!" she cried.

Asta spent the day in her cave. As evening drew in, she stood beneath the troll queen's window, playing with her golden apple.

"Give it to me!" the troll queen called from her window. "What will you give me in return?" asked Asta.

51

"You may visit the prince tonight," the troll queen replied.

But again there was no waking him. And, as soon as morning came, she was dragged from the castle by the troll queen's guards.

With one last gift to use, Asta stood beneath the troll queen's window once more. Her golden pear glinted in the pale light of the northern sun.

"You may see the prince tonight," gloated the troll queen, "in return for that shining pear."

"But it'll be the last time," she added, "for tomorrow we marry and then he'll be *mine*."

That night, like the others, the prince slept like one enchanted. Then it came to Asta how she might break the spell.

Hidden within the folds of her clothes, was the candle her mother had given her so long ago. She lit it and watched three drops of hot wax fall onto the sleeping prince...

With a start, he woke.

Chapter 6

The spell breaks

"You've come just in time," the prince cried. "I was to marry the troll queen tomorrow night, but you've found me before the year is out."

Then, from the stone turret, came the sound of heavy feet.

"Hurry! We must flee," urged Asta. "The troll queen is coming."

As she spoke, the first light of dawn pricked the night sky.

"I am still a bear for
one more day," roared
the prince.

Turning, Asta saw he was a
white bear once more.
"Climb on my back," he said.

58

As the troll queen opened the
bedroom door, the bear charged
past her down the turret stairs.

"Come back!" she cried.
"Never," snarled the bear.
"Stop them," the troll queen
ordered her guards.

But the trolls were no match for
the giant bear. With one swipe
from his paw he scattered them
like leaves, then burst through the
castle door.

Together, Asta and the bear
galloped to the icy shore. There, a
boat bobbed on the water. In one
bound, the bear leaped aboard.

"I thought you would need
help escaping," said the North
Wind. "All this time I have been
resting. Now I will take you home."

For months, they journeyed south,
the North Wind blowing the boat
as gently as he could.

"I have lost my riches," the prince told Asta. "All my treasure is trapped in the troll queen's castle."

"She can keep it!" laughed Asta. "I know of a beautiful farmhouse where we can live..."

When at last they stepped off
the boat, Asta turned to the North
Wind and asked, "Why did you
and your brother winds help me?"

"Your story was foretold to us,"
the North Wind replied. "For you
are the girl who went to the ends of
the earth for love."

East of the Sun, West of the Moon is a fairytale from Norway. It was collected by two writers, Peter Christen Asbjørnsen and Jørgen Moe, in the nineteenth century, and put into their famous book of Norwegian folk tales.

Designed by Helen Edmonds
Series designer: Russell Punter
Series editor: Lesley Sims

First published in 2009 by Usborne Publishing Ltd., Usborne House, 83-85 Saffron Hill, London EC1N 8RT, England. www.usborne.com
Copyright © 2009 Usborne Publishing Ltd.